THIS BOOK BELONGS TO:

The Little Kipper *Collection*

Honk!
Arnold
Splosh!
Sandcastle

*Hodder
Children's
Books*

A division of Hodder Headline Limited

Honk!

Mick Inkpen

'Honk!' said the gosling.

'Where did you come from?' said Kipper.

'Honk!' said the gosling again.

'You can go in the
bath!' said Kipper.
'Honk!' said the gosling
to the plastic duck,
which didn't reply.

'Do you like
    bubble bath?'
said Kipper.
    'Honk!' said the gosling,
blowing a bubble
    by accident.

'Can you only say
Honk?' said Kipper.
The gosling nodded.
And honked again.

It honked
   at the towel.
It honked
   at the sponge.
It honked
   at the hairdryer. . .

E specially when
it blew him
out of the bathroom!

And it honked
as it bumped
into Big Owl!
'Are you all right?'
said Kipper.

But the gosling
didn't reply.
It didn't say 'honk'.
It fell fast asleep,
without saying
anything at all!

Arnold

Mick Inkpen

Pig arrived at Kipper's house with his little cousin Arnold.

'Will you look after my little cousin for a while?' he said.

'Hello Arnold,' said Kipper.

Arnold stared at Kipper and sucked his thumb.

'Come on Arnold,'
       said Kipper.
'You can play with my toys.'
       Arnold followed Kipper,
sucking his
thumb.

'Which one do you like best?'
said Kipper.
But Arnold just
looked at the toys,
and carried on
sucking his
thumb.

'Do you like Rabbit
or Big Owl?'
said Kipper.
    Arnold sucked his
thumb.

'How about Slipper?
Or Sock Thing?
Or Mr Snake?' said Kipper.
Arnold took his
thumb out. . .

. . . then put it
back again.

'Hippopotamus is good!' said Kipper. 'Look, he can squeak!'

'Squeak! Squeak! Squeak!' went Hippopotamus. . .

. . .while Arnold sucked his thumb.

Suddenly Arnold STOPPED
sucking his thumb.
He went to the toybox,
and looked inside.
'Is THAT what you
like best?' said Kipper.

So Kipper made his
toybox into a
little house for Arnold,
who seemed pleased. . .

. . .and started sucking
his thumb again.

Splosh!

Mick Inkpen

'Splash!'
went the rain
on Kipper's umbrella.

'Splosh!' went the puddle as Kipper jumped into it.

'FLASH!' went
the lightning.
'BOOM!' went
the thunder.

'Drip, drip, drip,' went the water off the hedgehog's nose.

'Hop, squelch!
Hop, squelch!
Hop, squelch!'
went the three
little rabbits.

'A A A TISHOO!'
went the hedgehog.
And then he did it
again!
'ATISHOO!'

' Slop slap!
    Slop slap!'
went the water
under the umbrella.

And at last,
   without a slap,
or a slop, or a hop,
   or a squelch, or a drip,
or a boom, or a flash
   or a splosh,
      or a splash. .

. . . out came the sun!

Sandcastle

Mick Inkpen

Kipper was making
sandcastles.
It wasn't easy.
The first one wobbled
and fell over. The second
one crumbled at the corner.
But the third one
was just right.

Kipper made a big
     pile of sand and
patted it smooth.
     Then he dug,
and piled, and patted
some more. And this is
what he made.

A seagull landed on
Kipper's castle.
It squawked and flew
away again.
'That's what I need!'
said Kipper.
'Something to
go on top!'

Kipper found some
     seaweed and some
pebbles.

'No, they won't do,'
he said.

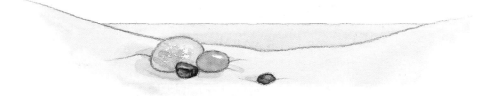

He found a shell.
It was pink and pointy.

'Perfect!' he said.

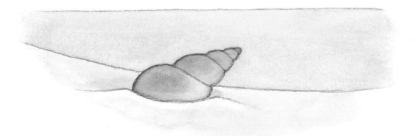

Kipper put the pink
and pointy shell on
his castle.

But the pink and pointy
shell got up and walked
away . . .

. . .there was a little
crab inside!

So Kipper stopped
building his sandcastle.
He bought himself an
ice cream, and a sticky
lolly too!

  While he was licking
the last bit of lolly,
an idea
popped into
his head.

He stuck the cone on the castle and the sticky lolly wrapper on the sticky lolly stick.

It looked even better than the pink and pointy shell. . .

. . .don't you think?

Other Kipper books

KIPPER

KIPPER'S TOYBOX

KIPPER'S BIRTHDAY

KIPPER'S SNOWY DAY

KIPPER'S CHRISTMAS EVE

KIPPER'S BOOK OF COUNTING

KIPPER'S BOOK OF COLOURS

KIPPER'S BOOK OF OPPOSITES

KIPPER'S BOOK OF WEATHER

THE LITTLE KIPPERS

WHERE, OH WHERE, IS KIPPER'S BEAR?

KIPPER STORY COLLECTION

British Library Cataloguing in Publication Data

A catalogue record for this book is available from the British Library.

ISBN 0 340 84444 2
10 9 8 7 6 5 4 3

Text and illustrations copyright © Mick Inkpen 1998

The right of Mick Inkpen to be identified as the author
of this Work has been asserted by him in accordance
with the Copyright, Designs and Patents Act 1988.

Honk!
Arnold
Splosh!
Sandcastle
first published in 1998

This edition first published in 2001
by Hodder Children's Books
a division of Hodder Headline Limited
338 Euston Road London NW1 3BH

Printed in Hong Kong

Goodbye!